Save our Playground

For Yolanda who could be Yolanda
and for John-Jo who could be Alfie

Save Our Playground was first published in Great Britain by
HarperCollins Publishers in 1994

1 3 5 7 9 10 8 6 4 2

HarperCollins Children's Books is a division of
HarperCollins Publishers Ltd,
77-85 Fulham Palace Road,
Hammersmith, London W6 8JB

Printed and bound in Great Britain
by HarperCollins Manufacturing Ltd, Glasgow

ISBN hb: 0 00 185601-4
ISBN pb: 0 00 674851-1

SAVE OUR PLAYGROUND

LEON ROSSELSON

Illustrated by Anthony Lewis

Collins
A Division of HarperCollins*Publishers*

Contents

NOWHERE TO PLAY

The children's playground on the estate was falling to bits and everyone said there was no money to repair it. Martin and Liza could see it from the bedroom window of their fifth-floor flat. The chains that held the car-tyre seats for the swings were rusting and broken. Half the steps that led up to the top of the slide were missing. The see-saw was stuck in a horizontal position and wouldn't move at all. There wasn't one climbing frame that didn't have something broken or missing. The gate was now locked and a notice outside warned children that it was dangerous to enter the playground. It was a sad sight, especially on this dull November

Saturday morning.

"What a dump!" Liza exclaimed, staring out of the window. "Nowhere to play. Nowhere to go."

"Yeah," Martin said. He was more interested in strumming chords on his guitar. He'd been learning for six months and, with patience and hard trying, had managed to persuade his fingers to hold down three chords. Now, sitting on his bed, he was concentrating hard on getting his fingers round an E7. When he knew four chords properly, there'd be hundreds of songs he'd be able to play.

"No money, that's what they say. That's what they always say."

"Yeah," Martin said. His little finger on the second string wouldn't stay where it was put.

"It's not fair," Liza complained. "It's just not fair."

"Yeah," Martin said, his head bent over the guitar.

"Yeah. Yeah. Can't you say anything else?" Liza yelled, exasperated.

Martin managed to persuade his little finger

to stay where it was put and stroked his thumb down the strings to sound an E7 chord.
"Yeah!" he said triumphantly.

Liza threw a pillow at his head. He grinned and strummed a D chord rhythmically. "Come back, Liza, Come back, gal," he sang.

Liza joined in: "Wipe the tear from your eye. "It's serious, though," she said. "Somebody should do something. And if you say 'Yeah' again, I'll strangle you."

Martin laid his guitar down gently on the bed. "What can we do?" he said. "We got no money."

"We got no money," mimicked Liza. "Well, OK. But we got hands. We got voices. We got brains."

Martin was about to chime in with another 'Yeah', but thought better of it. He knew his sister's quick temper.

"Some of us have, anyway," she added, looking meaningfully at her brother.

"Well," he said, ignoring the insult, "we could raise some money."

"Good," said Liza. "How?"

Martin frowned and looked thoughtful. "I got four chords off now," he said finally. "We could go busking. Outside the supermarket. Cheer all those misery-face shoppers up. With your voice and my guitar playing, we'd make a stack of money. We could buy ourselves a whole new playground."

For a moment, Liza's eyes were bright with hope. Then she hunched back into gloom again. "Nah," she said. "Wouldn't work. Can you see our mum letting us go and busk in the streets?"

"We needn't tell her," said Martin.

"*We* needn't," she said. "But somebody else would. We wouldn't last five minutes. Anyway," she continued, "it's probably against the law. Mostly everything is."

Martin was silent. His sister was right. She usually was. They'd never be allowed to do it.

"Wait a minute," Liza said, brightening up again. "I've got a better idea. Why don't we put on a show?"

Martin made a face. "Wouldn't be much of a show," he said. "We only know one song properly. We'd have to sing it over and over to fill up the evening."

"Don't be daft," Liza said impatiently. "We'll learn more songs. We'll get other kids on the estate to do things."

"Who? How?"

"We'll advertise. We'll have auditions. We'll pick the best ones to be in the show." There was no stopping her now. She was bouncing up and down with excitement. "Then Christmas time, we'll put on this splendiferous show in our community centre and people'll come from everywhere and we'll charge them – I don't know – lots of money and it'll be a sell-out and that's how we'll get the children's playground repaired."

"If you say so."

Liza didn't seem to notice his ironical tone. She was carried away by enthusiasm. "Come on," she said. "The first thing is to write out the notices. We'll put them up all round the estate."

"What notices?"

"Haven't you been listening? Announcing the audition. We'll have it tomorrow. I expect they'll be queuing up to be in our show, but we'll only choose the very best."

Martin still looked doubtful but he knew better than to argue. Once his sister had an idea like that buzzing about in her head, she wouldn't listen to reason. She'd chase that buzzing idea to the ends of the earth and if it led nowhere, as it often did, she'd just give a shrug and say: 'Oh well, anyway, we tried.'

"Paper, coloured pencils. What are you waiting for, dozy?" Liza could see it already. The meeting house packed with people. The expectant hush before the curtain rose. The wild applause at the end. The audience standing and cheering. All the performers taking a bow. And she and her brother the stars of the show.

"Better get a dictionary as well," she added. "We don't want to spell words wrong. It's probably against the law to put up notices with wrong spellings."

They sat at the kitchen table with a set of coloured pencils, a pile of paper and a dictionary. They decided twenty notices would be enough. They'd do ten each.

"Look up 'audition'," ordered Liza. "I think I know how to spell it but—"

"OK, big sis," said Martin. He was used to being ordered about by his sister. He didn't really mind it. He was a good-natured boy. He opened the dictionary in the middle and looked vaguely at the words beginning with the letter O.

"It begins with A, little bruv," said Liza.

"I know, I know. Just testing you out," Martin said.

When Mrs Williams came home from shopping at midday, she was surprised and pleased to see her children sitting quietly at the kitchen table hard at work with paper and coloured pencils. Not even watching the telly, she thought to herself. She was always a little anxious when she had to leave them alone, even though Mrs Perkins in the flat next door was happy to keep an eye on them. Bringing them up hadn't been easy since her husband had died, but now they were growing tall and straight and she was proud of them even if they did get into mischief from time to time.

"Doing some crayoning?" she asked.

"Yes, Mum," Martin replied.

"That's what I like to see."

She put her shopping bags down and went to look at what they'd done. She picked up one of the notices and read:

AUDITION AUDITION AUDITION. FOR THE WHEELBARROW ESTATE XMAS SHOW. CHILDREN WANTED WHO CAN SING DANCE JUGGLE PLAY AN INSTRUMENT. COME TOMORROW SUNDAY 8 NOVEMBER AT 2.30 TO 51 WILLOW COURT.

The notice was decorated with multi-coloured children singing and dancing.

Mrs Williams frowned. Liza and Martin looked at her questioningly. Would she approve?

"What's this about a Christmas show?" she said.

"We're going to put it on in the community centre," Liza explained. "We're going to raise lots of money so we can get our playground repaired."

"I see." Mrs Williams was doubtful if this venture would raise any money at all, let alone enough to repair the playground, but she didn't want to discourage them. "Whose idea's that?" she asked.

"Mine," Liza and Martin said together.

"And who said you're going to be able to use the community centre?"

"Can't we?" Liza asked anxiously.

"You'll have to ask the committee."

"Can't you ask them?" Liza said.

"I might. But what about the audition now? This notice says it's at 51 Willow Court. That's where I live."

"Yes, Mum," Martin said happily.

"Well, I don't remember anyone asking me to use my place for children to sing and dance and juggle and play instruments and goodness knows what."

Martin opened his mouth to say something but no words came out.

"We've done all these notices now," Liza said. "It took us hours. Can't we?"

There was a moment's tense silence. Then

their mum said: "I'm going to see your Uncle Willie tomorrow afternoon. His back's playing him up again, poor man. When I come back, I want to see this place spick and span and no mess. You understand?"

"No problem," said Liza.

Martin jumped up and gave his mum a hug and a squeeze.

"Now you can help me unpack the shopping," Mrs Williams said.

"But, Mum, we've got to put these notices up," Liza objected.

"First shopping," Mrs Williams insisted. "Then you can put up your notices."

The main courtyard of the estate was a grassy square around which cars were parked. Signs on the surrounding walls warned:

NO BALL GAMES
and
BALL GAMES ARE NOT ALLOWED
ON THE LAWN OR ON THE
ESTATE ROADWAYS

That afternoon, children on the estate were intrigued to find an assortment of colourful notices sellotaped underneath the signs. By the end of the afternoon, all the notices had peeled off and were fluttering about the courtyard. All except for the one Martin and Liza had stuck on to the KEEP OUT sign outside the children's playground. That stayed there until late Saturday night when Vince Malleson, coming back from the pub where he'd had more to drink than was good for him, decided he'd like to try out the slide in the playground, tried to climb over the gate, lost his footing, grabbed the notice as he fell, tearing it off the gate, and landed with a bump on his head in the mud. When he woke in his own bed the next morning with a splitting headache, he had no idea how he'd got there or why he was clutching a bedraggled piece of paper inviting him to an audition at 2.30 that afternoon.

THE AUDITION

"What we'll do," said Liza, "is we'll make everyone wait in the sitting room and we'll be in the kitchen and we'll ask them to come in one at a time and do their act and we'll give them marks out of ten—"

"Suppose nobody comes," Martin interrupted.

"Course they'll come. There's hundreds of children on this estate. They'll all want to be in the show, won't they? We probably won't be able to squeeze them all in. You'll see."

At 2.30 on Sunday afternoon, Liza sat at the kitchen table, a pen and a blank sheet of paper in front of her, feeling both nervous and important. Martin waited near the front door, ready to answer it when the bell rang. At three o'clock, Martin went back into the kitchen to report.

"Five," he said. "Natalie, Alfie, Wobble, Yolanda and a little girl I don't know. I think she's new."

"Is that all?" asked Liza.

"Told you."

"I expect there'll be others coming later."

"I expect there won't," Martin said. "We'd better start. Otherwise Mum'll be back before we've finished."

Liza bit hard on the end of her pen. "Miserable lot," she said. "All right. Call the first one in."

Martin went into the sitting room and returned leading a small girl by the hand. Then he took his place next to Liza at the kitchen table.

"Name?" rapped out Liza. She was irritated now. It wasn't turning out quite as she had hoped.

The small girl said nothing and her face was pink.

"What's your name?" Martin asked more gently.

The small girl opened her mouth and whispered something.

"Didn't hear you," said Liza.

"Cheryl," said Cheryl in a small voice.

Liza wrote it down carefully.

"What do you do, Cheryl?" she asked.

Cheryl looked baffled.

"Do you sing, dance, juggle?" Martin explained.

"Sing," said Cheryl in a tiny voice.

Liza wrote it down.

"All right," she said. "We're ready."

They waited. Cheryl looked at them, looked at her feet, looked at them and turned even pinker.

"Come on, Cheryl," said Martin, trying to give her confidence. "Sing something."

"Loudly, so we can hear you," added Liza. "Some hopes," she muttered under her breath.

Silence.

Liza was losing patience. "Sing, Cheryl," she ordered.

Cheryl closed her eyes, took a deep breath, opened her mouth and sang. The voice that came out was so loud Liza and Martin almost fell off their chairs. It was a warm voice, too, and perfectly in tune. They were impressed. But what was she singing?

"I love the sun

It shines on me—"

"Hymns," said Martin. "She's singing hymns."

"God made the sun—"

"Wait a minute," Liza demanded.

"And God made me."

"Thank you, Cheryl," said Martin.

But eyes closed tight, hands clasped together in front of her, Cheryl sang on defiantly, ignoring their attempts to stop her.

At the end of the second verse, Cheryl took a breath.

"Thanks, Cheryl," said Liza, "but—"

"I love the rain," Cheryl's voice burst out again. "It splashes on me—"

Liza put her head in her hands.

Cheryl ploughed on relentlessly through the third verse, the fourth verse, the fifth verse, while Martin and Liza sat, hands over their ears, powerless to stop her.

As soon as the hymn was finished, Cheryl opened her eyes and said in an indignant little voice: "It's rude to interrupt people when they're singing."

"Sorry, Cheryl," Martin said. "But we don't really want hymns. We get enough of that at school."

"Don't you know anything else?" asked Liza.

Cheryl shook her head.

"Well, you've got a good voice," said Martin brightly, wanting to encourage her. "Hasn't she, Liza? Hasn't she got a good voice?"

"Oh yeah," Liza said. "Loud. She's got a loud voice all right."

Cheryl beamed.

"As long as it's not singing hymns," Liza went on. "As long as it can learn another song."

Martin led Cheryl back to the sitting room

and returned with a boy who was almost as wide as he was tall. His bottom wobbled noticeably when he walked, which was how he got his nickname.

"Name?" asked Liza.

"Sylvester Brown," said Wobble.

Liza wrote 'Wobble' on the paper.

"What are you going to do for us, Wobble?" she asked.

Wobble took half a dozen balloons out of his pocket and with the utmost seriousness proceeded to blow them up. Liza and Martin watched, hardly believing their eyes.

"Wowee!" exclaimed Martin. "This is exciting."

"The audience'll go berserk when they see this," said Liza. "Ber-serk."

Wobble finished tying a knot in the neck of the last balloon, threw the six differently-shaped balloons in the air and bowed solemnly.

"Is that it?" asked Liza. "Is that all?"

Wobble took another balloon from his pocket and threw it on the table in front of them. "You do it," he challenged.

Martin took the balloon and blew into it till his chest heaved and his eyes bulged but he made no impression on the balloon.

"Give it here," said Liza. She too blew till she was pop-eyed and breathless but the balloon remained defiantly limp and unblown-up. Liza tossed it back to Wobble who, with seemingly no effort, blew it up until it assumed the shape of Mickey Mouse, tied a knot in the neck and threw it in the air.

"You've got a talent for blowing up balloons, all right," admitted Liza.

"But will people want to see it?" asked Martin.

"Could you do it on ice?" Liza wondered. "Or roller skates? Or standing on your head?"

Wobble shook his head.

"Oh well," said Liza. "Wait in the sitting room. Who's next?"

"Natalie," said Martin. "Send her in, Wobble."

Natalie was carrying a recorder.

"Name?" asked Liza.

Natalie giggled. "I'm Natalie," she said.

"You know I am."

Liza wrote it down.

"I suppose you're going to play the recorder," Martin said.

"How did you guess?" said Natalie.

"Go on, then," said Liza, writing 'recorder' down on the paper.

They watched her as she put the recorder to her lips. As she took a breath and prepared to blow the first note, she giggled. She took a breath and tried again. Again she giggled.

"Sorry," she said. "It's 'cos you're looking at me."

Liza made a despairing gesture. "What are we supposed to do?"

"I can't play if people are looking at me," Natalie said. "I just can't."

They stared at her.

"Could you turn round?" asked Natalie. "Could you face the other way?"

Martin and Liza looked at each other. This was becoming ridiculous. They turned their chairs round so that they faced the window. Natalie, after a few fluffs and false starts, played her recorder piece flawlessly.

"Finished," she said. "You can look now."

Liza and Martin turned their chairs back again.

"We can't ask the audience to turn round when you're on stage," Liza said. "They'll think we're mad."

"It's just that my breathing goes all funny when people are watching," Natalie said.

"Oh well," said Liza. "We'll think of something. Call the next one."

The next one was Alfie Roberts. He was carrying a battered instrument case, out of which he produced an old ukelele.

Martin looked at it with interest. "You going to play that?" he asked.

"What do you think?" said Alfie.

"Where did you get it?"

"I found it in the cupboard. My great-grandad used to play it."

"Name?" demanded Liza.

"I don't know," Alfie said.

"You don't know your name?"

"I don't know my great-grandad's name,"

Alfie retorted.

"No, I mean *your* name. That's what you're supposed to do at auditions. They ask your name and you tell them."

"Who said?"

"Alfie!" Liza admonished him.

"Anyway, you know my name. You've just said it."

Liza gave an exasperated sigh and wrote down "Alfie". Then she sucked the end of her pen. "What's that instrument?" she asked.

"A ukelele," Alfie said proudly.

"How do you spell uke – whatever it was?"

"U-K-E for short," said Alfie.

Liza wrote it down. "Go on, then," she said. "Surprise us."

Alfie hung the strap of the ukelele round his neck, took a plectrum in his right hand, placed the fingers of his left hand on the strings, pushed his left foot forward as if he was about to start a race and began: "Any old iron, Any old iron, Any any any old iron—"

The problem was that what he was playing on the ukelele seemed to have nothing to do with what his voice was singing. He was rattling the strings happily with his plectrum, putting his fingers anywhere up and down the ukelele. He didn't seem to notice that it didn't fit the tune, that Martin wore a pained expression on his face, that Liza had her fingers in her ears.

"I wouldn't give you tuppence for your old watch and chain, old iron, old iron."

He signified the end of the song by thrashing a particularly loud discordant sound on the instrument.

Martin squealed with pain.

"What's wrong with you?" Alfie demanded belligerently.

"It's the chords, Alfie. They're not right."

"What chords?"

"What you're playing on the ukelele. Didn't anyone teach you any proper chords?"

"I don't know anything about chords," Alfie said suspiciously.

Martin and Liza looked at each other.

"Oh well," said Liza for the third time. "Wait in the sitting room."

"You sang the song well, anyway," Martin told Alfie, as he was putting the ukelele back in its case. "Didn't he, Liza?"

"Terrific," said Liza flatly. "What was it?"

"Dunno," said Alfie. "I learned it off my dad."

Alfie departed and Yolanda entered carrying a cassette recorder. She wore a long red dress down to her ankles.

"Name?" asked Liza.

"Yolanda," said Yolanda.

"What are you going to do, Yolanda?"

"Dance," said Yolanda.

"This had better be good," muttered Liza, writing it down. "Otherwise I might throw myself out the window."

Yolanda pressed the start button on the recorder. Pulsating music blared out. Yolanda swayed on to her right foot, then on to her left foot, then back on to her right foot. She twitched her shoulders. She wiggled her hips. She swirled round and round, her long dress billowing outwards. She shook her shoulders. She jerked her hips from side to side. Liza and

Martin had never seen anything like it. Yolanda switched the machine off.

"Great," said Liza. "What was it?"

"Salsa," Yolanda said.

"Never heard of it," Martin said.

"That's what they dance in Cuba."

"Thanks, Yolanda," said Liza. "Wait in the sitting room."

When she'd gone, Liza asked: "Do you think she was making that up? Salsa and all that?"

Martin shrugged. "I dunno. Funny sort of dance if you ask me."

"Well, we'd better go and tell them the good news," Liza said without enthusiasm.

"We forgot to give them marks out of ten," said Martin.

"You must be joking," she said.

VINCE TRIES IT ON

"Congratulations," Liza said to the five children waiting patiently in the sitting room. "You've all been chosen to be in our show to raise money to mend the children's playground."

Everybody clapped.

"Only—" she went on.

"Wait a minute," interrupted Alfie. "Who said you could be in charge?"

"It was our idea," Liza said. "We thought of it."

"Well, we haven't seen you audition, have we? We haven't seen what you're going to do in this show."

There were murmurs of support at the stand Alfie was making, especially from Wobble who was still smarting at the suggestion that his act was boring.

"Fetch your guitar, little bruv," Liza said. Martin brought his guitar from the bedroom and strummed the D and A7 chords to make sure he was going to be able to change the position of his fingers quickly enough. Then, as sweetly as they knew how, they performed their party piece, "Come Back, Liza". Liza sang the verses and they both sang the choruses, Martin joining in with a harmony. There was a moment's silence, followed by a burst of applause. There was no doubt about it. Liza and Martin were good, even Alfie had to admit that.

"As I was saying," Liza said, flushed with success, "we're going to put on this show in the community centre. Our mum's going to ask if we can use it. It's to raise money to pay for mending the children's playground 'cos at the moment we've got nowhere to play. We're all going to be doing our acts *but—*" she said emphatically, "there's gonna have to be some changes. Alfie, you've got to learn some chords on your uke."

"I told you," Alfie argued. "I don't know anything about chords."

"Well, you've got to find someone who can teach you to play it properly. Like your great grandad did."

"He's dead," objected Alfie.

"Well there must be someone who isn't dead who could teach you." Liza wasn't in a mood to accept any arguments. She was in charge and that was that. "Cheryl," she went on, "you've got to learn to sing songs not hymns. All right?"

Cheryl turned pink but agreed silently.

"Natalie—"

"I know," said Natalie. "I've to learn to play when people are looking at me."

"Correct," said Liza. "Now, Wobble, we've got to think of something to make your act more exciting."

Wobble looked glum.

"He could do it to music," suggested Martin. "He could move to music while he's blowing up balloons."

They all looked at Wobble and shook their heads. The idea of Wobble moving gracefully to music was too far-fetched.

"Everybody thinks it's easy blowing up these balloons," Wobble complained. "But it isn't. Even my dad can't do it."

"That's an idea," said Liza. "You could give the balloons to people in the audience to try and blow up and when they couldn't do it, they'd see how hard it was and then you'd do it easily—"

"And if Wobble blew up so many balloons, all different shapes and sizes, and filled the stage with them—" chimed in Natalie.

"Like soap bubbles," said Alfie. "How about that? I could blow soap bubbles at the same time. I'm the champion soap-bubble-blower."

"And I could make up a balloon and bubble dance," offered Yolanda excitedly.

"Sounds good," Liza said. "What else?"

"We should finish the show," Martin said,

"with everyone singing and playing instruments."

"And dancing," added Yolanda.

"Yeah, all right. I'll play guitar and Alfie'll play ukelele and Natalie'll play recorder and Liza and Cheryl'll sing and Yolanda'll dance and—"

"I can't sing," admitted Wobble.

They all turned to look at him.

"I can't," said Wobble. "Listen." He stood up and began to chant in a tuneless monotone. "Twinkle, twinkle, little star, How I—"

"Stop!" everyone yelled.

"That's what they say at home," Wobble said sadly. "Whenever I sing anything, they all scream at me."

"Never mind," said Martin. "There must be an instrument you can play."

"Like what?"

"What about drums?" Martin suggested.

"Haven't got any drums," Wobble said mournfully. "Haven't got any instruments."

"Has anyone got any instruments Wobble could play?" Liza asked, taking charge.

They all shook their heads. Then Alfie said: "We used to have a broom handle."

"A what?" Liza exclaimed.

"It had bottle tops on it," Alfie explained. "You get a broom handle and you get lots of bottle tops, like beer bottle tops, then you hammer nails through the bottle tops into the broom stick and when you shake it, it rattles. My dad made one. He said he used to play one in a band once. He showed me it."

"Can you borrow it for Wobble to play?" asked Liza.

"We haven't got it any more. My mum threw it away. She said she was fed up with seeing it. My dad wasn't pleased. They had a row about it."

"I could make one," Wobble said. "I'm good at making things."

"You get a broom handle," Alfie said again, "and you get loads of those metal—"

"I know," Wobble interrupted. "You just said that. It's all right. I can make it. I've made a model aeroplane. And a model boat. And a coffin for my hamster when he died. So I reckon I can make that all right. I'll play the broomstick and blow up balloons. That's what I'll do."

He seemed content now that he'd found something else he could contribute to the show.

"That's settled, then," said Liza, relieved. "We'll all join in at the end. It'll be the grand finale."

"What'll we sing?" asked Yolanda quietly.

"We'll think of something," Liza said. She was becoming anxious. Their mum would be home any minute.

"It should be about the children's playground," Martin said. "We should make up a song about saving the children's playground."

Everybody thought that was a good idea. So it was agreed. They would practise their acts at home. They would rehearse every Sunday afternoon and write a song for the grand finale.

"You'd all better go," Liza advised. "Our mum'll be back soon and she wants everything spick and span when she comes home."

Before anyone could leave, there was a ring at the door. Martin went to answer it. Vince

Malleson was at the door. He wore a baseball cap back to front and was bleary-eyed and unshaven. His fall from the gate of the children's playground the night before had raised an angry red bump on his forehead.

"What do you want?" Martin said.

Vince ignored him and pushed past into the sitting room.

"Is this the audition?" he demanded, waving the tattered piece of paper he'd torn off the playground gate.

"It's only for children," Liza replied. "You're too old."

"Wait a minute," Vince said, pulling behind his head at his baseball cap. "I haven't come to audition. What I want to know is – who's your manager?"

"What manager?" Alfie demanded.

"There you are then," Vince said. "You're only kids. You'll never manage by yourselves. You need a manager. In other words, my little darlings, you need" – he punched the air with his fist – "me."

There was a moment's stunned silence.

No one knew what to say. They were all more than a little nervous of Vince Malleson. Finally, Yolanda broke the silence.

"What's a manager do?" she asked in a low voice.

"Manages, of course," Vince replied. "Organises. Makes sure everything runs like clockwork. Sorts out problems. And all for ten per cent of the takings."

"What!" exclaimed Natalie.

"Oh no," Liza burst out indignantly. "That money's not for you, that's for mending the children's playground."

"Now look—" Vince began.

"We don't need a manager," Martin interrupted. "We can manage ourselves. And if we did want a manager, we wouldn't choose you, Vince Malleson."

Vince took hold of Martin by his middle, lifted him off the ground and turned him upside-down. "You sure of that?" he asked.

"Help!" cried Martin.

"Put him down!" yelled Liza, furious, and aimed a vicious kick at Vince's calf.

Vince yelped, dropped Martin in a heap on the floor and turned towards Liza, wagging his finger at her. "Watch it!" he warned. "I eat little girls for breakfast."

"You'd better go," Liza shouted defiantly. "Our mum'll be home any minute and she'll eat you for tea."

Some of the children laughed. Vince glanced nervously at the door. One person he didn't want to meet was Mrs Williams. He'd felt the lash of her tongue more than once before.

"You wait," he blustered, retreating from the room. "You haven't seen the last of me. Don't say I didn't warn you." And making a rude sign at them, he went out slamming the front door behind him.

A cheer went up from the children.

"You all right?" Liza asked, as Martin picked himself up.

"Good job he dropped me on the carpet," he said.

"What will he do?" asked Natalie.

"He won't do anything," Liza said. "We won't let him." She looked at Cheryl, pinker than ever now and trembling slightly, and put her arm round her.

"It's all right, Cheryl," she said comfortingly. "Everyone knows Vince. He's harmless really. He's all talk. Isn't that right?" She looked around for confirmation from the other children.

"Yeah," they all agreed, but not very confidently.

"Rehearsal here next Sunday at half-past two," Liza announced. "Don't be late."

WOBBLE AND THE BOTTLE TOPS

Wobble's first problem was where to find a broom handle. There was one in the cupboard, naturally, but it was attached to a broom and was frequently used to sweep floors. Wobble wasn't altogether sure his step-mum and his dad would approve if it disappeared one day and turned up the next decorated with bottle tops. It wouldn't matter, of course, it could still be used as a broom handle – at least, when he wasn't playing it as an instrument – but still, parents were funny like that. They might not understand. They might stop his pocket money and he needed his pocket money to buy more balloons.

Wobble, whose mother had died, lived with his father, his father's new wife, his grandmother, who was his first mother's mother, and his baby brother, whose mother was Wobble's second mother. He also had numerous uncles, aunts and cousins who lived nearby and who were always visiting. All of them fussed over Wobble's baby brother, chucking him under the chin and throwing him up in the air and declaring to one another that they had never seen such a delightful baby. He was everyone's favourite, Wobble's baby brother was. He was named John and Wobble was named Sylvester and that, Wobble thought, wasn't fair for a start.

On the Tuesday morning after the audition, Wobble was sitting at the breakfast table in the kitchen finishing a slice of toast and honey. He was almost ready to leave for school. His dad had already gone to work. His grandmother was still in bed in the room she shared with Wobble. His mother was in the bathroom.

Wobble, as he'd been told to, was keeping an eye on his baby brother who was sitting in his high chair eating from a bowl of dry coco pops. Suddenly, his baby brother, grinning at Wobble provocatively, tipped the bowl upside-down so that the coco pops poured on to the floor. He was always doing things like that and he never got into trouble for it.

"Mum!" shouted Wobble. "John's spilt all the coco pops again."

"Sweep it up, would you, darling?" came his mother's voice from the bathroom. "There's a good boy."

It was then that Wobble had what he thought was a bright idea. He put the open jar of honey at the edge of the table so that his brother could reach it. Then he went out slowly to fetch the broom from the cupboard in the hallway. When he returned, John was holding the jar between two chubby hands and inspecting it with his head cocked on one side. Wobble swept the coco pops into a neat pile, then leaned the broom against the table just where his brother usually dropped things. John was beginning to turn the jar of honey upside-down.

"Come on, John," urged Wobble. "Do it!"

He went out again for the brush and pan. As he came back to the kitchen he heard a crash and ran to the table. It was better than he'd hoped. The jar of honey was on the floor, broken, and honey was oozing everywhere and especially on to the broom. To be on the safe side, Wobble plunged the head of the broom into the sticky mess. John bounced up and down, gurgling happily.

"Oh no!" yelled Wobble. "Look what John's done."

His mother came running from the bathroom, wiping her hands on a towel. "What was that crash?" she asked. Then she saw the mess on the floor and groaned.

"It was John," Wobble explained. "He's always doing things like that."

"Why did you let him do it, Sylvester?"

"I was getting the brush and pan," Wobble said innocently. "I didn't know he could reach the honey."

His mother inspected the honey and the broken glass on the head of the broom. "How am I going to get this clean?" she said.

Wobble's heart sank. Surely she wasn't going to—

"No," he heard his mother say. "About time I bought a new one anyway. Throw this one out."

Wobble breathed a sigh of relief. "Can I have the broom handle?" he asked quickly.

"What for?"

"To make something with."

"Make something, make something," his mother muttered. "Always making something, this child."

"Can I?"

"You're not going to do dangerous things with it?"

"Course not."

"Well, OK. But we'll have to leave this now or you'll be late for school. I'll clear it up when I get back."

She lifted John out of his high chair and threw him up into the air. He screamed with delight.

"Naughty boy," she said lovingly.

So he'd solved one problem. But the problem of the bottle tops remained. Where was Wobble going to find them? He had tried looking in rubbish bins and dustbins until a rat had scuttled out of a dustbin when he lifted the lid off. After that, he decided to avoid dustbins. He hadn't found any bottle tops there anyway, only masses of cans and other more disgusting things.

By Friday, he was becoming disheartened. The broomstick, wiped clean, was carefully hidden underneath his bed, but the bottle tops seemed as far away as ever. He might as well be looking for buried treasure. And he so much wanted to bring the instrument he was going to play to the Sunday rehearsal.

That evening, to his surprise, his father came home carrying two crates of beer. Wobble ran to look. It was a miracle. His heart danced with joy. They were the right sort of bottles with the right sort of bottle tops, enough surely – when nailed on to a broomstick – to make a lovely rattling noise.

"Who's going to drink all that?" he asked his father.

"This? This is good beer, this," said his father. "It's for your Aunt Hortense's party tomorrow. It's her birthday. Fifty years old, she is."

"That's old," said Wobble.

"That's special," said his father. "It's going to be a big, big celebration."

"Can I come?"

"No room for little 'uns," said his father. "No, you're staying home to look after Gran and John. And Alice'll be in to give you your tea."

"Can I have the bottle tops, then?"

"The bottle tops?"

"From the bottles. I need them. All of them."

"What do you want bottle tops for?"

"To make something."

"What something?"

"Something special."

"Always making something, this one is," said his father and pinched Wobble's cheek.

"Can I?"

His father scratched his head. "I don't know.

If I remember and if they're not thrown away first, I'll try and bring some home. But I can't promise."

Wobble turned away glumly. That wasn't good enough. He knew what would happen. They'd forget all about it. Or they'd just bring back two or three. They never took what he said seriously.

That night, he lay in bed for ages listening to his grandmother's heavy breathing. Sometimes she snored and sometimes she coughed so hard she woke him up. And sometimes she got up in the middle of the night and wandered around as if in a dream.

"She doesn't know what she's doing. It's like she's sleepwalking," his mother had explained.

His grandmother snorted and sat up in bed.

"Who's that?" she said in an alarmed voice.

"It's me, Grandma. Sylvester."

"Sylvester?" She stared in his direction as if trying to remember who he was. "I didn't see you come to bed."

"You were asleep, Grandma."

"Asleep?" She lay back on the pillow. "I

wasn't asleep. I never sleep."

"Never, Grandma?"

"Sleep for ever soon enough."

"Shall I get you a drink of water, Gran?" He always said that when he didn't understand what she was saying or when she seemed agitated. It seemed to calm her.

"There's a good boy."

He brought a glass of water from the kitchen. She sipped a little and put the glass on her bedside table, next to the cup with her false teeth in. He scrambled back into bed.

"What's that stick for?" she asked suddenly.

He looked at her, surprised. "What stick, Grandma?"

"That stick. Underneath your bed. Why do you put sticks underneath your bed?"

How did she know that? He was sure she'd been asleep when he'd put it there. Maybe she saw more than she let on.

"It's to make something," he said.

"Make something, make something," she grumbled. "Always making something, he is."

Then there was silence and soon he could

hear her heavy breathing again. Surely she was asleep now. But *he* couldn't sleep. His mind was buzzing. Bottle tops, bottle tops, bottle tops rattled inside his head. That's all he could think of. Would they remember to bring back all the bottle tops? They wouldn't, he knew they wouldn't. They'd forget and then excuse themselves by saying that they didn't think it was that important. And, of course, it wasn't important to them. But it was to him. If he lost this chance, he might never have another. He'd never be able to make this instrument which he so much wanted to play in the children's show. He could see himself on stage with the other children, the audience applauding, his parents so proud. He had to have that instrument. He just had to. Bottle tops, bottle tops, bottle tops went his brain.

It was no good. He couldn't sleep. He slipped out of bed and padded to the kitchen for a drink of water. The crates of beer were next to the fridge. He stroked his finger over the hard cold metal tops on the bottle. He liked the feel of them. He liked their golden colour. He wanted them. He so much wanted them.

There was a bottle opener in the drawer. It wouldn't matter if he opened one bottle, if he took one bottle top just to see what it was like. It was a moment's work to prise the bottle top off. It felt fine in his hand. He looked at the crate of bottles. One bottle without a top looked silly when all the other bottles had their top hats on. As if in a dream, without really meaning to, he opened another bottle, then another, then another. Soon all the bottles in one crate were open and a small hill of bottle tops stood on the floor in front of him. He gasped and put his hand to his mouth. What had he done? He hadn't meant to do it. How had it happened? Well, it was too late now.

He took a plastic bag, scooped all the bottle tops into it, tiptoed back to his room and hid the bag under his bed. Then he went back to the kitchen and contemplated the crate of opened beer bottles. What was he to do? Perhaps, if he poured the beer down the sink, they'd think that burglars had broken in and drunk the beer. They did that, burglars did.

He'd heard about it somewhere.

He took a bottle from the crate and sniffed it. It had a funny smell. But his father had said it was good beer. He put the bottle in his mouth, took a swig and nearly choked. It tasted awful. Bitter and sour. Worse than boiled cabbage and he hated boiled cabbage. He poured the rest of the bottle down the sink. He did the same to bottle after bottle. He'd almost emptied all the bottles in the crate when he heard a sound and froze. Someone was coming into the kitchen. He must have woken his father up. And his father was going to be furious. Wild with fury. He was going to— No, he didn't even want to think about it. What could he do? There was no time to get back into bed. He'd be spotted. But he had to escape somehow. He'd better pretend to be still asleep. That was the only thing he could think of doing.

When Wobble's father shone his torch into the kitchen, his heart missed a beat and his skin went cold. There lying in a sprawled heap on the floor, lit by the torch beam, was his son, Sylvester, seemingly unconscious. His father ran over to him and shook him.

"Sylvester, what's the matter? Wake up!" he said in an agitated voice.

Sylvester's eyes remained heavily closed. He began to snore.

"Wake up!" his father said again.

There was no response from Sylvester.

His father sniffed the air. What was that funny smell? He shone the torch around the kitchen. The beam focused on the crate of empty beer bottles.

"What the—!" He bent over Sylvester, caught a whiff of beer on his breath and yelled out in panic: "Quick! Mira! Come here! Call the police! Call the ambulance! Sylvester's drunk a whole crate of beer."

Sylvester's mother came running. His baby brother, startled by the noise, began to scream furiously. His grandmother emerged from the bedroom muttering to herself: "A body can't get any peace and quiet in this house."

"Oh, my poor darling!" exclaimed Wobble's mother.

"What do you mean, poor darling?" shouted

his father. "He's only drunk a whole crate of beer. A whole crate of my best beer! Phone for the fire brigade!"

"Try and wake him," cried his mother as she rushed to the phone.

At this point, Sylvester decided it might be a good idea to put an end to this scene before the police, the ambulance and the fire brigade became involved. Eyes still closed, arms outstretched, he rose to his feet and, as his parents watched open-mouthed, took slow measured steps back to his bedroom.

"He's sleepwalking," said his mother.

"Sleepwalking, my eye!" said his father. He'd caught a glimpse of small pools of beer in the sink and was beginning to suspect what had happened.

Father, mother and grandmother followed Sylvester to the bedroom where he sank slowly into bed, still, to all appearances, in a deep unbreakable sleep.

"Will he be all right?" whispered his mother.

"Oh yes," replied his father grimly. "He'll be all right. Just wait till I see him tomorrow morning, that's all."

"Back to bed, Gran," said his mother. "Panic's over."

"Can't get any peace and quiet in this house," grumbled Gran.

"It's a madhouse, all right," said his father. "A madhouse."

The next morning, Wobble woke to find his father waiting for him at the breakfast table.

"Good morning," he said, hoping this show of politeness would soften his father's anger.

"Never mind good morning," said his father. "What about last night?"

"I don't remember," said Wobble.

"Never mind don't remember. What about that crate of empty beer bottles?"

"I don't remember," said Wobble.

"What about you lying on the kitchen floor smelling of beer?"

"I don't remember," said Wobble. "I don't remember anything."

"You don't remember? You don't remember emptying a whole crate of beer?"

"I must have been sleepwalking," said Wobble.

His father went into Wobble's bedroom and came back with a plastic bag. "What about this?" he said. "Full of bottle tops. How did this get under your bed?"

"I must have done it in my sleep," Wobble said. "I must have been sleepwalking. Gran does it sometimes. Honestly. I don't remember anything."

He met his father's hard stare with an expression of blank innocence.

"So who's going to pay for my crate of beer?" said his father at last.

Wobble sighed. "Me, I suppose."

"You, I suppose," said his father. "That means no more pocket money for the rest of this year."

"Oh, Dad! It's gonna be Christmas."

"So?"

"I need to buy presents," Wobble said. "Can't I pay for it out of next year's pocket money?"

His father thought for a minute. Then he said: "On one condition. You tell me what you want a broom handle and a bag of bottle tops for."

So Wobble told him. And what Wobble told him seemed to sweeten his father's temper. "So you're going to be in this children's show?"

"Yes."

"And you're going to make this instrument, whatever it's called?"

"Yes."

"You want to make it this afternoon?"

"Yes."

"You want me to help you?"

"Yes please."

"OK. On one condition."

"What's that?" asked Wobble.

His father wagged a stern finger at him. "You don't do any more sleepwalking," he said.

NATALIE PLAYS TO THE PIGEONS

Yolanda, clutching her tape recorder, came to call for Natalie on Sunday afternoon so that they could go together to the rehearsal. She wore her red dancing dress and was already swaying excitedly from side to side when Natalie answered the door looking glum.

"You ready?" asked Yolanda.

"I'll never be able to do it," Natalie said.

"Do what?"

"Play my recorder when people are watching. My hands shake and I can't breathe. Just thinking about it makes me nervous."

Yolanda followed her into the kitchen. There, sitting on a row of chairs, were all Natalie's old dolls and teddies. Yolanda thought they looked rather bored.

"I've been practising," Natalie explained. "I'm pretending they're an audience. But it's no good. I know they're not going to shout at me or laugh. So I can play to them all right."

"No one's going to laugh," Yolanda reassured her.

"And I can play to the goldfish," Natalie went on. "And to my kitten. Except she keeps climbing up my legs whenever I pick up the recorder. It's just people make me nervous. Especially grown-ups."

"Have you tried closing your eyes?"

"I can't play with my eyes shut. Anyway, it doesn't make any difference. I know they're watching me."

"What about your mum and dad?"

"They're reading the papers in the sitting room. I won't play if they're in the room."

"It'll be all right," Yolanda said. "Come on. Don't want to be late for rehearsal."

Natalie sighed. "I'll never be able to do it," she said. "I know I won't."

"You will," said Yolanda.

"Do you think so?"

"I know you will," said Yolanda.

And she sounded so confident, because she was by nature a hopeful girl, that Natalie almost believed her.

"We're going to the rehearsal," Natalie called to her parents.

"Be back before it gets dark," shouted her mother.

An army of pigeons had descended on to the grassy square outside and were squabbling with the sparrows over some bread that someone had thrown down.

"Play them a tune," suggested Yolanda.

"What?"

"Go on," urged Yolanda. "See if you can play to the pigeons."

"What for?"

"I bet you can't," said Yolanda.

"You're daft," said Natalie.

She put her recorder to her lips and started to

play. Some of the pigeons turned their beady eyes upon her. Others fluttered towards her as if expecting this piping sound to lead to food. The rest continued to peck at the bread.

"I knew you could do it," said Yolanda.

"They're pigeons," said Natalie, "not people."

"Some of them look like people," Yolanda said. "Look at that big fat pigeon over there bullying the little sparrow. Just like my brother."

"It's no good," said Natalie. "I know they're not people."

They turned towards Willow Court where Liza and Martin lived and nearly collided with a dishevelled figure wearing a back-to-front baseball cap. It was Vince Malleson. He grinned at them. Or rather sneered.

"Going somewhere?" he said.

They stared at him, saying nothing.

"Wanna sell that old machine?" he demanded, pointing to Yolanda's tape recorder.

Yolanda shook her head.

"Give yer a penny for it," he said and

laughed. Or rather cackled.

Yolanda shook her head.

Suddenly, Vince stopped laughing and bent down over them so that his face was just inches away from theirs.

"I know where you're going," he said. "And you tell 'em from me – ten per cent. Or else."

"Or else what, Vince?" asked Yolanda.

"Don't you be cheeky," he warned. "You just tell 'em. From me. Ten per cent. Or else. Got it?"

And he slouched away.

"You're late," said Liza when she opened the door to them. "Cheryl and Alfie have been here for ages."

"Natalie played a tune for the pigeons," explained Yolanda.

"And we met Vince Malleson," added Natalie.

"And he said to tell you," Yolanda said, "ten per cent or else."

"Or else what?" asked Martin.

Yolanda shrugged. "He didn't say."

"He can't do anything," Liza asserted. "Our

mum's asked the committee if we can use the community centre and they said we could and they're going to give us tickets to sell, so what can he do?"

There was a moment's silence while all of them contemplated the awful things that Vince Malleson could do.

The ring at the door startled them. Martin ran to answer it, first looking through the letterbox to make sure it wasn't Vince. But it was only Wobble.

"You're late," said Liza.

Wobble took no notice. He lifted up his new broomstick instrument triumphantly and rattled it. A cheer went up. Wobble looked so proud you'd think he was going to burst. He passed it round so everyone could have a go at shaking and rattling it.

"Look," said Liza at last. "We'd better start this rehearsal. Our mum wants this place spick and span when she comes back from Uncle Willie's so there's no time to mess about."

"What about the biscuits?" asked Martin.

"Afterwards," said Liza. "Two each when

we've finished rehearsing. She baked them for us."

They all looked at her, waiting for her to tell them what and how to rehearse. Liza hesitated. She wasn't sure what was supposed to happen in a rehearsal. But she was in charge so she'd better get on with it.

"Me and Martin are practising a new song," she said. "What about you, Cheryl? Have you learned a song yet?"

Cheryl turned pink, looked at her feet and shook her head.

"It's all right," Martin intervened. "We know lots of songs. We'll teach you one. I'll play the guitar for you if you like."

"Thank you," Cheryl mouthed silently.

"Alfie?" Liza rapped out.

Alfie looked at his battered ukelele case and shrugged. "I asked my dad," he said. "But he said he didn't know anything about ukes. He said he'd try and find out when he had time."

"And when's that going to be?" Liza asked, exasperated.

"Dunno. He's always working."

Liza looked as if she was about to tear her hair out. "You've got one more week," she said. "Otherwise—" She left the threat unfinished. "How about you, Natalie?"

"I'm – um – I don't know," stammered Natalie. She was too nervous to admit that she still couldn't play to an audience in case Liza shouted at her.

"She played to the pigeons," said Yolanda, trying to be helpful.

"Oh, that's all right then," Liza said sarcastically. "We'll just have to make sure we have an audience of pigeons, won't we? How about sparrows? Shall we ask a few sparrows along as well?"

Natalie looked as if she was about to cry. Martin groaned. He knew his sister's quick temper could ruin everything. Yolanda flushed. She had to say something, anything, to rescue the situation.

"You don't understand," she said. "All Natalie's got to do is pretend everybody's a pigeon. Then she won't be nervous."

"How's she going to do that?" asked Liza.

"Imagination," said Yolanda. "I mean we all look a bit like pigeons. You're a tall, thin pigeon and Wobble's a little fat pigeon and Alfie—"

"No, I'm not," objected Alfie.

"Come on, Natalie," urged Yolanda, taking charge. "First of all, take deep breaths. I've just remembered. That's what my dancing teacher used to tell us. 'Take deep breaths to calm your nerves, darlings.' That's what she told us. Then just pretend we're all pigeons."

Natalie looked bewildered. She put the recorder to her lips but her hands were trembling so much she couldn't keep her fingers over the holes.

"It would help," Yolanda said, "if everybody waved their arms about and made pigeon noises."

There was an embarrassed silence. Then, to everyone's amazement, Cheryl crouched down, flapped her arms and began to coo. After a moment's hesitation, the other children followed suit. Soon the room was alive with children being pigeons, flapping their wings and pecking at the ground and cooing and clucking and squawking.

Yolanda put her hand on Natalie's arm reassuringly. "Come on, Natalie. You can do it. Play the pigeons a tune."

Then she, too, became a cooing, flapping pigeon.

Natalie breathed deeply and as she breathed she saw that her hands were becoming less trembly. She closed her eyes for a moment. She heard cooing and clucking and squawking sounds. She saw pigeons all around her gazing up at her with their beady eyes. One more deep breath and she opened her eyes and began to play. After a shaky start, the music flowed out confidently. Natalie was concentrating so hard she heard nothing but the tune she was playing, so she didn't notice that the pigeons had stopped cooing and clucking and squawking and flapping their wings and were listening entranced. When she'd finished, there was a burst of pigeon-cheering. Then the pigeons stood up and became children again.

"No problem," said Liza.

Yolanda turned a somersault. "I knew you could do it," she cried.

Natalie gave a pleased smile. Suddenly, she felt nervous again. Would she be able to play like that in the community centre with all those people watching? Her heart started to beat faster just thinking about it. She took a deep breath. Well, maybe she would. She'd done it once so she could do it again.

"All you've got to do," said Yolanda, as if reading her thoughts, "is take deep breaths and pretend all the people are pigeons."

"No problem," said Liza again. "What else?"

"This song we're going to sing at the end," Martin said. "What about that?"

"That's right," said Wobble. "We've got to write a song about the children's playground."

"How do you write a song?" asked Alfie.

"Well," said Martin who'd been giving some thought to the matter, "I think we should take a song everyone knows and put new words to it."

"What song?" asked Natalie.

"Something simple," said Martin. "So I can

play it on my guitar."

There was a silence as they all tried to think of a song.

"London Bridge is falling down," sang Yolanda suddenly.

"Good idea!" exclaimed Liza. "Then we can change it to 'The children's playground's falling down, falling down, falling down. The children's playground's falling down, my fair lady'."

"What's my fair lady got to do with it?" asked Alfie.

"Nothing," admitted Liza.

"How shall we mend it?" suggested Yolanda.

"That's it," said Liza.

"Put new chains on the swings, on the swings, on the swings," sang Martin.

"Put new chains on the swings," everybody joined in.

There was a pause.

"That's how we'll mend it," sang Martin suddenly, completing the verse.

"Better write this down before we forget it," said Liza.

Soon everybody, even Cheryl, was contributing ideas for verses and Martin found he only needed two chords to be able to accompany the song on his guitar and Wobble enthusiastically shook and rattled and banged his bottle-top broomstick and Alfie beat out the rhythm on his ukelele case and Yolanda improvised a children's play-ground dance and they were all singing away at the tops of their voices and having so much fun and making so much noise that they didn't notice Mrs Williams until she was standing stern-faced at the sitting-room door.

The noise and the singing died away. They looked at her anxiously.

"Oh, Mum." Liza put her hand to her mouth. "We haven't finished rehearsing yet."

"I can see that," said Mrs Williams. "You call this spick and span?"

"Sorry, Mum," Martin said. "We forgot the time."

"I see," said Mrs Williams. "Have you children had your biscuits?"

They shook their heads.

"Take two biscuits each from the tin in the kitchen," she said. "Then off you go home before I have your parents round here saying I've kidnapped you all."

"Same time next Sunday," yelled Liza to the children as they rushed into the kitchen for their biscuits.

When they'd all gone, Martin gave his Mum a hug and asked: "Are you cross with us?"

"I should be," she said.

But he could see that she wasn't.

And what she didn't say was that she'd been standing outside the front door for ages listening to the sound of their singing with a smile on her lips and even a tear or two in her eyes.

ALFIE AND THE UKELELE MAN

Alfie had passed the shop many times before. It was just round the corner from the estate, a few doors away from the chip shop. Until he'd found his great grandad's ukelele, he'd never given it a second glance. But now whenever he walked past it, he stopped to stare into the shop window, letting his eyes linger on the dusty-looking instruments displayed there: guitars and banjos, mandolins and autoharps and violins and a ukelele much like his. It wasn't a prosperous shop. Everything about it was old and shabby. The name over the shop front, Markham's Musical Instruments, was so faded you could hardly read it.

On Monday after school, he took a detour to pass the shop again and peer through its grimy windows. The instruments were still there. Nobody had bought them. So far as Alfie could see, nobody ever bought anything in Markham's.

He was standing there, trying to summon up enough courage to go in when the shop door opened and a man peeped out. Alfie prepared to run. Most shopkeepers were suspicious of small boys staring through their windows. But this shopkeeper gave him a friendly smile. He was a stout man, quite old, with a bald head and a round jolly face.

"Thinking of buying something?" he asked.

Alfie shook his head.

"No money?"

Alfie shook his head.

"That's the trouble nowadays," said the man. "People with money don't want to buy and people who want to buy don't have the money. Am I right?"

Alfie nodded in agreement.

"Well, there's no point in standing out there in the cold," continued the man. "Better come in."

Alfie followed him into the shop. More instruments were displayed on the walls. There were racks of guitar strings and banjo strings and mouth organs and tuning forks. There were sheets of music, some so old they were curling at the edges. Everywhere was dusty and messy and Alfie loved it. He felt at home. He wanted to stay there for ever.

"Is this your shop?" he asked.

"It is," said the man. "I'm the one and only Maurice Markham. And who might you be?"

"Alfie," said Alfie. "Alfie Roberts."

"That's a good name," said Mr Markham. "I knew an Alfie Roberts once. Played the concertina. Maybe he was a relative of yours?"

Alfie shook his head.

"Well, pleased to meet you, Alfie Roberts," said Mr Markham, holding out his hand.

Alfie shook it solemnly. "I've got a ukelele," he said.

"Have you indeed? And where did you get that from?"

"It was my great grandad's."

"Must have been," said Mr Markham. "Very popular it was in your great grandad's day. Such a simple instrument, you see, the ukelele. Everybody played it. Not any more," he said sadly. "It's all electric guitars nowadays. Am I right?"

"I want to play it," Alfie said.

"Really?"

Alfie nodded vigorously.

Mr Markham beamed. "Where do you live?"

Alfie told him.

"Nip off home then. Come back with your ukelele double quick and we'll see what we can do."

Alfie was out the door and halfway home almost before Mr Markham had finished speaking.

"Where have you been?" his mother asked when he arrived home breathless.

"Nowhere," he gasped, ran to the cupboard, grabbed the ukelele and was sprinting out of the front door when his mother yelled at him: "Where do you think you're going?"

"Gottlearnplayuke," Alfie gabbled as he ran down the stairs.

"Alfie!" his mother screamed after him. "Come back here! What about your tea?"

But he was gone.

His mother sighed and shook her head in despair. "That boy!" she exclaimed. "He'd try the patience of a saint."

"No need to rush, lad," Mr Markham said as Alfie tried to catch his breath. "I'm not going anywhere. Not yet a while anyway. Now let's see what we've got here."

Alfie handed him the ukelele in its case. He took the instrument out and looked it over. "Not bad," he said. Then he peered at the strings, stroked his finger across them and sucked his breath in sharply. "Are these the same strings your great grandad played?" he asked and winked at Alfie.

"Don't know," said Alfie.

"Well, let's see if we can find some new ones."

He opened a drawer behind the counter, took out a packet of strings and began to replace the old ones, humming to himself while he worked.

Alfie's face wore a worried frown. "I've got no money," he piped up.

Mr Markham looked at him and grinned. "That's the way it is nowadays," he said. "Those that want to buy have got no money. Didn't I tell you?"

Alfie nodded.

"Never mind. You can pay me back when you're a famous ukelele player. Agreed?" And again he winked at Alfie.

"Yes, Mr Markham."

"Like George Formby. Did you ever hear of George Formby?"

Alfie frowned. "Don't think so."

"'When I'm Cleaning Windows'. Know that one?"

Alfie shook his head.

"What songs do you know then, Alfie?"

"I know 'Any Old Iron'."

"Do you now? Let's hear it then."

So Alfie sang it to him, the bit that he knew.

"Well, I never. Who taught you that?"

"My dad."

"Well, it may surprise you to know, young Alfie, that I, Maurice Markham, used to sing that song. Famous for it, I was. In my day. Of course, the man who launched it, as it were, the man who made it famous was the celebrated, the one and only Harry Champion. Ever heard of him?"

"Does he live round here?" asked Alfie.

"Doesn't live anywhere any more, Alfie. Although maybe he does in a way because I remember him as if it was yesterday. I used to go and see him perform when I was a lad not much older than you. Harry Champion. He was the champion, all right. Looked a bit like me, too. A jolly man with a red nose. And what energy. He used to rattle out that song at a rare old speed."

"I've got to sing it for our show," Alfie explained.

"What show's that?"

"We're doing it. Some children and me. On the estate. 'Cos our playground's falling to bits.

We've made up a song about it. But I don't know anything about chords and Liza said I can't sing it unless I learn chords. And I want to sing it."

"And you shall sing it, Alfie, you shall."

Mr Markham finished putting on the strings and began to tune them up. "I'm using the D tuning," he said. "Does that mean anything to you?"

Alfie shook his head.

"Never mind. It's an easy instrument. That's why it was so popular."

He handed the instrument back to Alfie.

"You'd better go home now. Alfie. Come back tomorrow and I'll teach you some chords. Agreed?"

Alfie's face fell. "Can't you teach me now?"

"Your parents are going to get worried if you don't go home now. Come back tomorrow. And look after this instrument. It's a bit of history you've got there."

His mother was waiting for him, her face like a dark cloud.

"What do you mean by running off like that?"

she demanded angrily. "Where have you been?"

Alfie was used to being shouted at. Whether he was at school or at home, he always seemed to be in trouble. And yet he never meant to do anything wrong. It was just that if there was a puddle of trouble to be walked into, he'd walk into it.

"I had to learn the ukelele," he explained.

"Learn the ukelele?"

"Mr Markham at the music shop said I could."

"Mr Markham? You went and asked Mr Markham . . .?"

"He said he'd teach me. He used to sing 'Any Old Iron'. He was a champion when he was my age and he had a red nose. And I'm going to be a champion, too, 'cos he's going to teach me chords."

His mother stared at him. "I don't think I know what you're talking about," she said. "Perhaps you'd like to explain properly."

So Alfie tried to explain properly, or, at least, as properly as Alfie could. He'd never been very good at explaining. Alfie's explanations usually left everyone more confused than before. But this time, his mother thought she more or less understood what had happened. And when she'd understood, she softened a bit. She knew how much Alfie wanted to play the ukelele. Ever since he'd discovered it in the cupboard he'd been badgering his father to show him how to play it. But his father was so busy these days, repairing cars all hours in his one-man garage. Finding out how to play the ukelele was the last thing on his mind.

"Next time, you just ask me," she said. "Rushing off like that. I've been phoning everyone on the estate trying to find out where you were."

"I've got new strings," Alfie said proudly. "Look!"

"Did you hear what I said?"

"Yes, Mum."

He opened the ukelele case to show his mother.

"Where did you get the money to buy those?" she asked.

"Mr Markham gave them to me. He said I

could pay him back when I'm famous."

"He'll have a long wait," said his mother. "I hope you thanked him. I hope you thanked him very very much."

Alfie nodded though he couldn't actually remember whether he had thanked him at all. But he certainly would thank him tomorrow. He'd thank him very very much.

"He's going to teach me chords tomorrow," he said happily.

"Alfie! What have I just said?" exploded his mother.

Alfie looked baffled.

"I said ask me if you want to go somewhere."

"Can I?" asked Alfie.

"Ask me tomorrow," said his mother.

The next day, after school, Alfie asked his mum, in a most sweet and polite way, if he could go to Mr Markham's for a ukelele lesson. She agreed, of course, and told him she'd come and collect him in an hour's time.

When Alfie arrived at the shop, Mr Markham was waiting for him. But it was a different Mr Markham. He didn't look the same. He wore a shiny black suit with a green tie and a waistcoat underneath. A black bowler hat covered his bald head. His oversize boots, too, were shiny and black. And his nose was red like a clown's. Alfie stopped open-mouthed as Mr Markham motioned to him to sit down on a chair. Then he sprang into action, launching himself into the chorus of 'Any Old Iron'. He sang it twice, once at the normal speed and once so fast, the words shot out like machine-gun bullets. Alfie thought it was the funniest thing he'd ever heard.

What's more, for the first time, Alfie understood what the words were about because Mr Markham accompanied the song with energetic actions. When he sang "Any Old Iron", he took a gold watch out of his pocket and pointed to it with an amused smile on his face. On "You look dapper from your napper to your feet", he put his hand on the top of his bowler hat and then pointed to his shiny boots. And when he sang "brand new tile", he took off his hat and waved it about.

At the end of the song, Mr Markham bowed

so low his bowler hat fell off and Alfie laughed and clapped so hard, he nearly fell off his chair.

"A bit of history," said Mr Markham, sitting down to recover his breath, "that's what that song is. Of course, there's a story in it as well. In the verses. You see, there was this chap whose Uncle Bill—"

"I've got an Uncle Bill," Alfie interrupted.

"There's a coincidence," said Mr Markham. "Well, this Uncle Bill died and left this chap his gold watch and chain. And did he show off! He thought he was so smart. He was the cock of the walk. But you see this watch and chain wasn't as valuable as he thought it was. In fact, it was rubbish. So everyone made fun of him for thinking he was so smart. Look, I've written the words of the first verse out for you. Do you think you can learn them?"

"Yes, please," said Alfie. "Thank you. Thank you very, very much."

"It's a pleasure, Alfie," said Mr Markham. "A real pleasure."

So Mr Markham taught him how to recite the first verse and then he said: "Now over the words of the chorus, I've put a number 1, 2 or 3. Can you see? That tells you what chords to play. When you see 1, you play chord 1. When you see 2, you play chord 2 and when you see 3, you play chord 3. Understand? So all you've got to do is learn three chords. Am I right?"

He took the ukelele out of its case and explained to Alfie how to make sure it was in tune. Then he showed him where to put his fingers to make chord 1. It took Alfie a long time before he could keep his fingers in position and press down hard so that the strings didn't buzz. But eventually he managed it and the bright, clear ripple of that chord as he brushed his fingers across the strings was, he thought, the most delightful sound he'd ever heard.

"Bravo!" exclaimed Mr Markham. "Now do you want to come back for chord 2 tomorrow or do you want to try it now?"

"Now," said Alfie eagerly.

Chord 2 was easier to learn because Alfie only had to press one finger down. And as his confidence grew, he made a successful attempt at chord 3 as well.

"He's got it!" exclaimed Mr Markham. "The boy's a genius."

Alfie blushed. He wasn't used to being praised.

"Now you go home and practise those three chords," Mr Markham said. "Use the plectrum to strum the strings. When you've learned them very well, try playing them while you sing the song. That's the hard part. But if you practise hard and if you persevere, you'll do it. Do you know what I mean – persevere?"

Alfie shook his head.

"We found a spider in our bath once," Mr Markham said. "We called him Percy. Percy Vere. Do you know why? Because no matter how many times he slipped back down the side of the bath, he still kept trying to climb out. That's what 'persevere' means. Keep at it."

Alfie wasn't sure if he'd understood what Mr Markham was trying to say but he couldn't ask because just then his mother arrived. His hour was up. Mrs Roberts raised her eyebrows in surprise when she saw Mr Markham with his red nose and funny clothes, but he welcomed her so nicely and praised her son so warmly, calling him the brightest boy, the politest boy he'd ever known, that she was quite overwhelmed. She had heard Alfie called many things but rarely bright and never polite.

"He's a credit to you, madam," Mr Markham said. "A credit to you."

Mrs Roberts thanked him.

"Come back and see me on Saturday, young Alfie," said Mr Markham. "Show me how you're getting on. Agreed?"

Mrs Roberts thanked him again and Alfie thanked him very, very much and then they both thanked him together. Just as they were going out the shop door, Alfie turned suddenly and asked: "Did he climb out the bath?"

Mr Markham looked startled. "What? Who?" he asked.

"Percy Vere."

"Ah – yes. Of course. He did, yes. Percy Vere. That's the word."

"What was that about?" his mum wanted to know when they were outside the shop.

"It's his pet spider," said Alfie. And that was the only explanation she could get out of him.

For the rest of the week, Alfie spent all his spare time practising the ukelele. It was driving his parents mad but they didn't say anything to him. They'd never seen him work so hard. So they smiled at him encouragingly when they saw him practise and put their fingers in their ears when they were out of sight.

"It could be worse," said his father. "He could be learning the violin."

By the end of the week, the ends of Alfie's fingers were sore but he could, if he concentrated very hard, almost change chords quickly enough to play the accompaniment to "Any Old Iron".

First thing on Saturday, he took his ukelele and set off for Mr Markham's music shop, not forgetting to ask his mum's permission first. He was looking forward to showing Mr Markham how much progress he'd made. But when he reached the shop, his face fell. Something was wrong. There was a metal grille over the windows. A "Closed" sign hung on the door.

He pushed at it but it was locked. He peered through the glass but there was no sign of Mr Markham.

Alfie stood outside the shop, kicking at the pavement, wondering what to do. He was disappointed and a little fearful, too. "Come back and see me on Saturday." That's what Mr Markham had said. So where was he? Had something happened to him?

A man who was cleaning the windows of the hardware store next door shouted over to him that the music shop was closed.

"I'm waiting for Mr Markham," explained Alfie.

The man walked over to him. "He's gone," he said.

"Where's he gone?"

"To a better world, I hope," said the man.

Alfie looked bewildered so the man continued: "He's passed over. Happened suddenly a few days ago. Heart attack. Died on the way to the hospital. Was it something important?"

Alfie didn't answer. He turned away, staring

at the pavement, his eyes blurred with tears. Then, clutching his ukelele tightly, he ran home.

"What on earth's the matter?" asked his mother when she opened the door.

Alfie said nothing. There was nothing he could say. He ran to his room and closed the door and there he threw himself on to the bed and wept silently into his pillow.

Then he dried his tears and stood up. He felt better. He thought of Mr Markham. He remembered him in his dusty music shop. He could see him still, singing 'Any Old Iron' with his jolly face and red nose, his gold watch, shiny black boots and bowler hat. He remembered the way he'd moved his hands and feet as he sang, performing all those funny actions that had made the song come alive for Alfie. And as he remembered, Alfie started to sing softly to himself: "Any old iron—" And he, too, though he had no watch or bowler, began to move his hands and feet, began to accompany the song with those same actions because they were a bit of history, they were, and he didn't want to forget them, ever.

"You look neat. Oh what a treat!
You look dapper from your napper to your feet.
Dressed in style, brand new tile
And your father's old green tie on;
But I wouldn't give you tuppence for your old watch and chain,
Old iron! Old iron!"

BREAKING THE SPELL

Liza and Martin were elated. The rehearsal had gone really well. They'd performed their new song, 'Jamaica Farewell', to enthusiastic applause from the other children, even though Martin had mixed up a few chords. Natalie had succeeded in playing her recorder piece yet again (to an audience of pigeon-children, of course). Wobble had blown up funny new balloons which he'd turned into sausage dogs. What's more he'd made everyone laugh by wobbling his bottom deliberately (as well as shaking his bottle-top broomstick) in time to the final song. Yolanda had invented two new dances. Alfie had been the biggest surprise of all. Even Liza had been impressed by his performance of "Any Old Iron", especially when he'd put down the ukelele and sung the final chorus very fast with all the actions.

As for Vince, nobody had seen him all week. They'd almost forgotten his threats.

So there was only one problem. Cheryl.

"She doesn't seem to want to sing anything but hymns," Liza complained. She was helping her mum make the tea. Martin was in the bedroom, strumming on his guitar. The other children had gone home.

"What's wrong with hymns?" her mother said. "A nice hymn is good for the soul."

"Oh, Ma!" Liza groaned. "She sang 'All Things Bright And Beautiful' today. Who wants to hear that?"

"If you've finished peeling the potatoes," said her mother, "you can lay the table."

"Why can't Martin do it?" objected Liza. "He never does anything."

"Argue, argue, argue," said Mrs Williams. "I say do this, she says she won't. I say do that, she says she can't."

"Well, it's not fair. I have to do everything."

"OK, OK. Tell Martin to help you lay the table."

When they were sitting round the table, eating their eggs and chips, the conversation again turned to the subject of Cheryl.

"We said we'd teach her a song," Liza said. "Didn't we, Martin? But she didn't seem to want to learn any of our songs. I think she's weird."

Her mother tut-tutted disapprovingly. "Just because she's shy," she said. "You have to talk to her, make her feel welcome."

"That's another thing," Liza went on. "She won't talk. She hardly ever says anything. Does she, Martin?"

"Got a good voice, though," Martin mumbled through a mouthful of chips.

"Well, I don't care," Liza insisted. "If she can't learn a proper song by next rehearsal, she's out of the show."

Martin frowned.

"She'll be upset," said her mother. "Have you

thought of that?"

"What else can we do? I'm just not having her sing miserable old hymns in our show."

"Go and see her," suggested her mother. "Talk to her."

"It won't do any good. Anyway, she never told us where she lives. And she doesn't go to our school."

"I know where she lives. Chestnut Court. Her father came to the residents' meeting at the community centre on Tuesday. Nice quiet man. Came up to me specially to thank me."

"What for?"

"For everything my children are doing for Cheryl. For bringing her out, that's what he said. Said Cheryl looked forward to the rehearsals more than anything. Said it was the best thing to happen to her since – since her mum left. That's what he said. Her father."

"Where's her mum gone?"

"That's all he told me. Best thing to happen to Cheryl since her mum left."

There was a silence. Martin stopped cramming chips into his mouth and gulped.

Liza sighed heavily.

"I thought this show was going to be fun," she said.

Liza and Martin went to see Cheryl the next day after school. She lived on Chestnut Court. Number 59.

"Why is everywhere on this estate named after trees?" Liza said. "'Cos there aren't any trees anywhere."

"I expect that's why," Martin said.

"That's daft," Liza objected. "There aren't any flowers either or wild animals. So why aren't they called Daffodil Court or Chimpanzee Court?"

Martin shrugged. He saw no point in arguing. Chestnut Court. Willow Court. Holly Court. They seemed perfectly good names to him. It was his sister who always argued about everything.

"What are we going to say to Cheryl?" he asked.

"We're going to ask her why she only sings hymns," Liza replied. "That's what. And," she added after a pause, "I'd like to know why she goes to Church Road School when we all go to Wheelbarrow Road."

"That's the school she went to before she moved to the estate," Martin said.

"So?"

"Perhaps she didn't want to change schools. It's a nicer school than ours anyway."

"No, it's not."

"That's what everybody says."

"Oh well, yes. They got trees, haven't they. They got gardens."

Liza was fed up with everybody saying rude things about their school and their estate. It wasn't fair.

They climbed the stairs to the fifth floor of Chestnut Court and stood outside number 59. They looked at each other. Then Liza took a deep breath and rang the bell. A small anxious-looking man answered the door.

"We've come to see Cheryl," Liza said.

"We're friends of hers," explained Martin.

The man looked at them, puzzled. Then a smile lit up his face.

"Liza and Martin," he said. "Cheryl told me about you. Come in."

He showed them into the sitting room. Everything was clean and neat and orderly. There were no books or games anywhere. Stranger still there was no television. They sat down feeling ill at ease. They didn't dare speak. It was as if the room itself disapproved of noise and talking. Cheryl's father continued to smile at them. Eventually he broke the silence.

"I'm Charlie Hutchinson, Cheryl's father," he said. "I met your mother last week. We had a long chat. I feel I know you already."

"We came to see Cheryl," Liza explained. She hoped it didn't sound rude.

"She'll be here soon," said Cheryl's father. "Her aunt's bringing her from school. She looks after her when I'm at work. Would you like some milk?"

Liza shook her head.

"She'll be very excited to see you," Mr Hutchinson went on. "She so much looks forward to your rehearsals."

"She's got a good voice," Martin said. It was

the only thing he could think of to say.

"She has that," Mr Hutchinson agreed. "Loves singing. Ever since she was a little tot. Always singing. Such a strong voice, too, for such a little one. Never talked much, no. But always ready for a song. In happier days. Of course, since . . . well . . . it hasn't been easy since everything changed. Her aunt's a great help. A saint, I would say. I don't know what I'd do without her. And you, too, of course. I'm very grateful for all you've done. Bringing her out. I told your mother."

Liza and Martin didn't know what to say. Mr Hutchinson seemed exhausted by the effort of making such a long speech. Another awkward silence seemed to be growing but then they heard the front door opening and Mr Hutchinson stood up immediately.

"That'll be them," he said.

When Cheryl saw them, she gave a jump like a startled rabbit and then went her usual pink colour. Her aunt looked at them and nodded, her face expressing distaste, as if they were making the room untidy. She was a bony, sharp-faced woman.

"Shouldn't you be at work, Charles?" she said.

"Just off." He turned to Liza and Martin. "Do come again. And give my regards to your mother."

And he was gone.

"Come into my room," Cheryl whispered.

"Tea in half an hour," ordered her aunt. "I'll want some help."

"Yes, Aunt Harriet," said Cheryl.

Once in her room, Cheryl seemed to relax. There was an old teddy on her bed and some books on a shelf on the wall. Also on the shelf was a framed photo of a young woman. She's pretty, thought Liza. They all three sat on the bed. Cheryl picked up the teddy and sat him on her lap.

"Who's that?" asked Liza pointing at the photo.

"That's my mum."

"Do you still see her?"

Cheryl shook her head. "Don't know where she is."

"Is that really your aunt?" Martin wanted to know.

"She's my mum's sister. She's nothing like my mum, though."

"Does she live with you?"

"No. Just looks after me when my dad's working. Sometimes he works in the evenings."

"Where does he work?"

"He looks after the car park. He used to be in an office. Then he lost his job. Then my mum left. Then he got this job. He doesn't like it, though."

She's talking, thought Liza. She's never talked that much before. Liza was working out in her mind how to tell Cheryl about not singing hymns when Martin intervened.

"Do you want us to teach you a song, Cheryl?" he said. "So you can sing it in the show."

Cheryl didn't answer at first. She hugged her teddy to her. Then, as if with a great effort, she said: "I know lots of songs."

Liza was taken aback. "Why won't you sing them, then?"

Again Cheryl struggled to answer. "I don't know," she said. "I can't explain." Then she added in a murmur, "I'm sort of scared."

"What of, Cheryl?" Martin asked.

Cheryl hugged her teddy but said nothing.

"Is it your aunt?" Liza asked. "Are you scared of your aunt?"

"I don't know," Cheryl said again. She looked at them. Her face was tense, anxious. They waited for her to explain. "She says it's sinful. She says God sees everything. She says God punishes sinners. She says—" She stopped and put her head in her lap. "I want to know why my mum left," she said in a low voice. "Maybe it was my fault."

Liza and Martin were stunned. They couldn't take this in. They'd never heard anything like that before.

"Cheryl!" Her aunt's voice cut through their thoughts like a knife.

"Yes, Aunt Harriet."

"I need some help, please. It's time your friends went home."

"I have to go," said Cheryl.

"What about your dad?" whispered Martin.

Cheryl shook her head. "He says now my mum's gone I have to do what my aunt says."

Liza and Martin walked home in silence, deep in thought. As they approached their own block of flats, Martin said: "Do you think God really sees everything?"

Liza was scornful. "Course not," she said. "How could he?"

"Maybe he's got special X-ray eyes that can see through walls and everything."

"Nah!" Liza shook her head knowingly. "God's invisible."

"He can't be," Martin said indignantly. "How can he be?"

"I suppose you think he's an old man with a long beard."

"If he was invisible," Martin argued, "how would anyone know he was there?"

"I don't know," Liza said irritably. She was tired of this argument. "What are we going to do about Cheryl?"

"We'll have to let her sing a hymn," Martin replied.

"Not if I can help it," Liza said.

They told their mother the problem as they were going to bed.

"It's like her aunt's a wicked witch," explained Liza, "and she's put a spell on Cheryl."

"And on her dad," added Martin.

"And as long as she's under the spell, she can only sing hymns."

"Even though she does know lots of songs," added Martin.

"I see," said Mrs Williams. "And you're going to break the spell, are you?"

"We're gonna try," said Liza.

But how? she thought to herself as she drifted off to sleep.

The days passed. Liza racked her brains trying to think of a way of breaking Cheryl's aunt's spell. In stories, a good fairy usually came to the rescue but if there were any good fairies still left in the world, they were unlikely to be living on the Wheelbarrow Estate.

"It's like she's frightened something awful's going to happen if she disobeys her aunt," Liza explained to Martin as they were walking to the baker's for bread and currant buns on Saturday morning.

"Like what?"

"I dunno. I suppose like her mum leaving or her dad losing his job."

"That wasn't her fault."

"Maybe she thinks it was."

"Weird," said Martin.

Just before they reached the baker's, Martin stopped suddenly and nudged Liza. "Look!" he said.

Then Liza saw her, too: Cheryl's Aunt Harriet crossing the road a little way in front of them. She wore a grey hat and a long grey coat and clutched her handbag close to her.

"Come on!" said Liza.

"Where to?"

"Let's follow her."

They kept twenty paces behind her, ready to dive into shop doorways in case she turned round. But she didn't look behind, nor to the right nor to the left. She marched purposefully past the baker's, past Markham's music shop, now boarded up, past the hardware shop and the chip shop. Then she stopped, took a quick look round and disappeared.

"She's gone into the betting shop," Liza said in amazement.

"Cor!" exclaimed Martin. "What a sinner!"

Liza grinned. "Yeah!" she said triumphantly. "Let's wait for her."

They waited. When Cheryl's aunt emerged, still clutching her handbag tightly, they planted themselves in front of her.

"We're Cheryl's friends," said Liza.

Aunt Harriet looked at them disapprovingly. "I know who you are," she said. "Have you been following me?"

"No. We just saw you go into the betting shop."

"We didn't think you'd go into betting shops," Martin added.

Aunt Harriet's face turned beetroot red, which didn't suit her. Grey was more her colour. For a moment she hesitated, looked as if she was going to push past them, then thought better of it.

"What do you want?" she asked.

"We want to know why you won't let Cheryl sing songs she wants to sing."

"Is that what she told you?" Aunt Harriet was taken aback.

"She's frightened you'll tell her off," Martin said.

"All I try to do," Aunt Harriet said coldly, "is teach her the difference between right and wrong. Something her mother seems to have forgotten."

"Well, she thinks you'll only let her sing hymns."

Aunt Harriet sighed. "The Lord's Day should be treated with respect. That is what I believe. I try to explain this to Cheryl. I try to explain that the Lord's Day is for worshipping the Lord, for singing songs that worship the Lord. The Lord's Day should not be profaned."

"What's 'profaned'?" asked Liza.

"You wouldn't understand," Aunt Harriet replied.

"I don't understand why you want to

frighten Cheryl," Liza said.

"I don't want to frighten her. I'm doing my best to help her father, poor man, that's all. And it hasn't been easy. However—"

She stopped as if uncertain how to continue. Liza and Martin sensed that she was weakening. They pressed home their advantage.

"We think you should tell her singing songs isn't sinful," Martin blurted out. "Even on Sunday."

"Not as sinful as betting on horses, anyway."

Aunt Harriet's face turned red again.

"So will you tell her it's OK to sing songs?"

"Release her from the spell, Aunt Harriet," Liza cried dramatically.

"The spell? What are you talking about?"

"I mean – tell her nothing awful's going to happen. Tell her she won't get punished."

Aunt Harriet sighed again. They waited for her to speak. "I'm not sure what ideas Cheryl has in her head," she said finally. "I certainly didn't intend to frighten her. To teach her the difference between right and wrong, that's all I've ever tried to do. However, perhaps I have been a little hard on her and I will try and do what you ask. And if I do," she continued, looking at them fiercely, "can I trust you not to tell Cheryl or her father about my – er – little weakness?"

"Oh yes," said Liza. "You can trust us all right."

"Definitely," said Martin.

Aunt Harriet nodded, adjusted her grey hat, pulled on her grey gloves and said: "A promise is a promise. God is watching you." And she marched away down the street.

"She gives me the shivers," said Liza.

"Do you think she'll keep her promise?" asked Martin.

"We'll see tomorrow, won't we?"

And they saw and they heard and it was indeed as if a spell had been lifted.

Cheryl was the first to arrive. She was beaming.

"Guess what happened yesterday," she said. "My aunt was really nice to me. She asked me to sing a song. She put her hand on my head and asked me to sing it. She said it's the sort of song I can sing even on a Sunday. I can't believe it. I thought she didn't like that song."

"What song was it, Cheryl?" asked Martin.

Cheryl composed herself, took a deep breath and sang in full, joyful voice:

"Somewhere over the rainbow, way up high
There's a place that I heard of once in a lullaby.
Somewhere over the rainbow, skies are blue
And the dreams that you dare to dream really do come true."

SAVE OUR PLAYGROUND

For weeks the children had been selling tickets for their show. They'd pasted up colourful hand-made notices everywhere they could. They'd been all round the estate. They'd tried selling tickets to teachers at school and even to customers in the local shops. A week before the show, a hundred tickets had been sold which was nearly as many as the community centre held.

"It's gonna be a sell-out," Liza told everyone.

She'd wanted to charge five pounds for the tickets but her mother had persuaded her to lower the price to one pound.

"People round here don't have much money," Mrs Williams told her. "And anyway, you're not big stars."

"We might be soon," Liza said.

Mrs Williams and Mr Roberts, Alfie's father, were going to be on the door.

"If they haven't bought a ticket, they can't come in," said Mrs Williams. "We don't want anyone barging in and causing trouble."

"And whatever you do," Liza warned, "don't let Vince Malleson in."

Mr Brown, Wobble's father, who was an electrician, was in charge of the lighting. Mrs Roberts and Mr Hutchinson had volunteered to be front of house, showing people to their seats. Yolanda's mum, who'd done a bit of amateur acting, was appointed stage manager. Her job was to look after the performers and make sure they knew when they were due on stage.

So it was that at four o'clock in the afternoon on the Sunday before Christmas, Liza and Martin, Yolanda and Alfie, Cheryl, Natalie and

Wobble were all standing on stage in their very smartest clothes, looking nervously out on to the empty hall, while Mr Brown adjusted the lights. The doors would open at four-thirty. The show was due to start at five o'clock.

They'd taken it in turns to try out their acts because Yolanda's mum said it was a good idea for them to get used to the stage.

"It's not the same as rehearsing in your front room," she explained.

And now Liza was worried. "We ought to have microphones," she said. "They'll never hear us. I mean they'll hear Cheryl. They'll hear Cheryl all over the estate but me and Martin can't sing like that."

"They'll be able to hear you perfectly well," said Mr Roberts. "As long as they're quiet."

"Suppose they're making a noise," said Liza. "Suppose they throw things."

"You're not going to be that bad, are you?" grinned Mr Roberts.

"And what about curtains?" Liza went on. "We ought to have curtains. It's not a proper theatre without curtains."

"You don't need curtains," said Yolanda's mum. "Just remember to enter stage right and exit stage left. And when you've finished your act give a little bow. Come on, now. You'll all be fine. Back to the dressing room. And relax."

They all trooped back to the dressing room behind the stage. Liza felt strange. Her mind was buzzing, her heart jumping. She was, she supposed, nervous. But also excited. She couldn't wait for the show to start. At the same time, she couldn't wait for it to be all over. She wondered if the others felt the same way.

She was the first to the dressing room and when she saw the notice on the door, she gasped. Scrawled in black biro on a scrappy piece of paper was: "Wotchout for Vince! Yah!!!"

"How did that get there?" she demanded.

"Vince must have put it there," Martin said.

"He couldn't have done. He couldn't have got in. The doors haven't been open. Somebody would have seen him."

"Unless he's made himself invisible," said Martin.

"That's all we need," Liza said.

Cautiously, she pushed open the dressing-room door and peeped in. It was empty. And there was nowhere for anyone to hide. They crowded into the dressing room. Wobble rattled his broomstick. Natalie tried out her recorder. Yolanda did a little dance in the centre of the room. Cheryl sat quietly in a corner. Martin made sure his guitar was in tune and then checked Alfie's ukelele. He'd discovered that Alfie knew the same chords as he did so they'd be able to play together in the grand finale. Alfie practised his three chords. Martin practised his four chords. Rattle, whistle, bang, strum. Liza sat there listening, clenching her fists, growing more and more tense and nervous, the noise swelling into a giant cacophony inside her head.

"Stop it!" she screamed. "It's driving me mad."

Everybody froze. There was a deathly silence which was worse than the noise. Nobody dared say anything. Then Yolanda spoke.

"Take deep breaths to calm your nerves,

darlings," she said in a funny voice.

Everybody laughed.

"I wish it was time to start," Wobble said. "How long do we have to wait?"

"I wish it was time to go to bed," said Natalie. "I feel sick."

Yolanda looked at her, smiled, crouched down and flapped her arms. "Coo, coo," she called.

Natalie grinned but inside she didn't think it was funny.

"Suppose Vince is in the hall," Martin blurted out.

"I don't even want to think about it," Liza said.

Time crept by.

There was a knock on the door. Yolanda's mum poked her head in. "Ten more minutes," she said. "Then Liza and Martin are on."

"What about the audience?" asked Liza.

"Full house. Don't worry."

And she was gone.

Five minutes later, she was back.

"Ready?" she asked.

Martin gave a last strum on his guitar. Then he and Liza followed Yolanda's mum to the stage. They stood at the side and listened to the hum of noise from the audience. Then the house lights dimmed and the hum faded into a whisper.

"Break a leg," said Yolanda's mum.

"What!" exclaimed Liza.

"It's what you say to performers before they go on stage. To wish them luck."

Liza and Martin walked uncertainly to the front of the stage. The lights dazzled their eyes. They couldn't make out anything in the darkness of the hall but they could sense the audience. They could almost hear the expectant silence. They could almost feel the eyes watching them.

It had been decided that Liza would welcome the audience to the show and explain why they were putting it on. She opened her mouth to speak but no sound came out. Her mouth was parched like a desert. Her mind seemed to have turned into a solid lump. She couldn't think of what she was supposed to say. She couldn't remember why she was there at all. If she had known it was going to be like this...

A scattering of laughs and titters rose from the audience. Liza and Martin felt their faces flush. Then they heard a noise behind them. The laughter spread. They turned round and went hot and cold. Vince was on stage behind them. He was wearing an old T-shirt and torn jeans, his back-to-front baseball cap on his head. He was thrashing an imaginary guitar and leaping from side to side like a demented rock star.

Liza was outraged. "Get off the stage this instant, Vince Malleson," she shouted. "This is our show."

He grinned at her. "Remember me?" he yelled, still thrashing his invisible guitar.

Yolanda's mum ran on to the stage and tried to pull him off but he pushed her away with a threatening gesture.

Some of the audience shouted for him to get off the stage. Others cheered him on. Arguments were breaking out in the hall. Vince was punching the air with his fist trying to lead the cheerers on.

Liza was furious. Her nervousness vanished completely. Vince was spoiling their show. She rushed up to him and aimed a sharp kick at his shin.

"Ouch!" he yelled.

He stopped pretending to play the guitar and made a grab for her.

She evaded his grasp and ran to the front of the stage. He leaped after her. Liza remembered the edge of the stage just in time and darted to one side. Vince, rushing forward, made another grab for her and, unable to stop himself, fell off the stage with a crash and a yell. There was a sudden silence. The house lights went up and everyone crowded forward to see what had happened. Vince was lying in a crumpled heap between the stage and the front row, his baseball cap half off his head.

"Is he dead?" someone said.

Vince groaned and sat up slowly, rubbing his head, a dazed expression on his face. Mrs Williams and Mr Roberts appeared at the front of the stage and stood over him, shaking their heads sadly. They took hold of his arms, helped him to his feet and led him out of the hall. He was still too dazed to resist.

There was a surge of laughter and chatter. After that, the audience settled back in their seats. They felt relaxed. They felt cheerful and friendly. They'd enjoyed that little episode. Now they were ready for the rest of the show.

Liza, too, found that her tension and nervousness had evaporated. She felt something like triumph. She'd defeated the giant, Vince. She could do anything.

As the house lights dimmed again and silence settled on the hall, she stepped into the pool of light on the stage and said: "Ladies and gentlemen, thank you for coming to our show. We're putting it on to raise money to mend the children's playground."

A few people in the audience clapped.

"The first thing is," Liza went on, "me and my brother, Martin, are going to sing a song called 'Come Back, Liza'."

There was more applause. Martin's fingers rippled over the D chord on the guitar. Liza, now full of confidence, started to sing.

The applause when they'd finished was deafening. Again they felt their faces flush, this time with pride. They both gave a little bow and hurried off the stage.

"Well done!" said Yolanda's mum. "On you go, Sylvester."

Sylvester wobbled on carrying a basket of balloons. He took one, blew it up and threw it into the air. A mocking cheer came from someone in the audience. Wobble took no notice. He blew up another balloon, then another and another, all different shapes and colours, until the stage was filled with floating balloons. Alfie appeared at the back of the stage and began to blow bubbles. Yolanda in her red dress danced on and began to twirl around the stage, pushing the balloons gracefully into the air and leaping high to catch the shimmering soap bubbles before they burst.

A balloon exploded with a bang which prompted a scream from the audience, followed by laughter. Finally, Wobble did his sausage dog balloon trick, bowed and wobbled off stage. The cheers that followed him were no longer mocking.

Alfie chased the balloons off stage leaving Yolanda to do her salsa dance while the audience clapped in time to the music. When she'd finished and the applause had died away, Cheryl, Alfie, Wobble, Martin and Liza joined Yolanda on stage. To giggles from the audience, they all crouched down and, arms flapping, began to hop about and coo.

"Throw them some bread," someone shouted.

Natalie walked on, breathing deeply. She felt sick. Her mind was in a panic. She couldn't even remember what piece she was supposed to be playing. The pigeon-children gathered in front of her, still cooing. She blew into the recorder. Out came a breathy whistle. The audience waited expectantly. She tried again. Out came a funny squeak. There was a tense silence. The children watched her anxiously, not knowing what they could do to help.

"They're only pigeons, Natalie," Yolanda called out.

Natalie pictured a flock of pigeons pecking bread in the grassy square of the estate. She'd played to them all right. She took a deep breath and raised the recorder to her lips. This time, the first notes were clear and a relieved sigh spread round the hall. Once started, Natalie grew in confidence, concentrating so hard she was hardly aware of where she was or who she was playing to.

At the end, she was so delighted and thankful to have got through it that she forgot to bow and ran off the stage the wrong side, the applause ringing in her ears.

Alfie grabbed his ukelele from Yolanda's mum, who was standing at the side of the stage, and walked into the spotlight. He blinked nervously. "Mr Markham taught me how to do this," he said. "I wish he was here but he's gone to a better world."

"What a shame!" someone shouted.

"Shush!" went the rest of the audience.

Alfie raised his face to the lights and recited:

"Just a week or two ago my poor old Uncle Bill

Went and kicked the bucket and he left
me in his will . . . "

When he'd finished reciting the verse, ukelele at the ready, he launched enthusiastically into "Any old iron, any old iron . . ." He didn't always get the chords right but it didn't matter because some people were joining in and others were clapping along in rhythm. Then he put the ukelele down and sang the chorus again, with all the actions, accompanied by laughter and cheers from the audience. Encouraged by this, he sang it again even faster and then again faster still, the laughter and singing, the cheers and the clapping getting louder all the time. By the time he'd waved to the audience and run, grinning, off stage, the place was in an uproar.

Cheryl's entrance was hardly noticed. Everyone was still laughing and talking excitedly about Alfie's performance and Cheryl was so small it was easy not to see her. She stood in the spotlight, staring at the front of the stage, growing pinker and pinker until a few people in the audience started hushing the rest.

Gradually, the hubbub subsided and there was silence. Cheryl raised her face and looked into the audience. She took a deep breath and began to sing:

"Somewhere over the rainbow . . ."

The soaring power of her voice shocked the audience. They couldn't believe that someone so small could sing like that. She sang with such feeling, too, such intense longing that everyone in the hall was on the verge of tears.

"If happy little bluebirds fly beyond
the rainbow
Why oh why can't I?"

There was a deep silence. No one wanted to break the spell. Cheryl looked at her feet. Then the hall erupted. Some people rose to their feet and others followed, clapping and cheering and whistling and shouting for more.

"That's what's called a standing ovation," Yolanda's mum said to Liza and Martin, who were with her at the side of the stage waiting to go on.

Liza felt a pang of jealousy at the response Cheryl was getting. But she also felt pride because, after all, if it hadn't been for her, Cheryl would never have managed to do it at all. She hoped Aunt Harriet was in the audience, even if it was a Sunday.

A very pink and pleased Cheryl walked off stage. Liza and Martin danced on and went straight into "Jamaica Farewell". Of course, everyone joined in the chorus and, full of high spirits now, clapped to the beat of the song. Liza didn't mind. She was happy. There was no doubt about it. The show was a success.

Then they were all on stage for the final song about mending the children's playground. Liza and Martin led it with Wobble shaking his broomstick and wobbling his bottom, Cheryl singing her heart out, Natalie conducting the audience with her recorder, Yolanda dancing round the stage and Alfie playing all the wrong chords on the ukelele. It didn't matter. By this time, nothing mattered. The audience were ready to applaud anything they did.

They followed that with another chorus that they'd written to the tune of "John Brown's Body":

"Save our playground 'cos we've nowhere else to play
Save our playground 'cos we've nowhere else to play
Save our playground 'cos we've nowhere else to play
Not next year, not tomorrow but today."

And then it was over. They stood on stage, their hearts beating wildly, beaming smiles on their faces, while everyone in the hall clapped and clapped.

The house lights went up. Mrs Williams climbed on to the stage and held up her hand for silence.

"I want to thank these children for the wonderful show they've put on," she said.

"Hear, hear!" shouted the audience.

"Maybe they haven't made us enough money

to repair the playground," she went on, "but they've done more than that. They've shown us the way. They've shown us that if we want something done, we've got to do it ourselves because if we wait for the people at the top to do it, we'll all be waiting till the Judgement Day."

"Right!" shouted the audience.

"But we've got no nice gardens for our children to play in so next week I'm calling a meeting so we can make a start on repairing this playground. Because our children need somewhere safe to play."

There was clapping and cheering and, because Liza couldn't think of what else to do, she started them all singing again:

"Save our playground 'cos we've nowhere
else to play
Not next year, not tomorrow but today."

The author and the publisher would like to thank the following for permission to reproduce copyright material.